ISBN 1 85854 601 X

Adapted with permission from THE WIND IN THE WILLOWS
by Kenneth Grahame © The University Chest, Oxford.
Published by Brimax Books Ltd, Newmarket, England, CB8 7AU, 1997.
Printed in China.

The Wind in the Willows

By Kenneth Grahame

Adapted by Lucy Kincaid

Illustrated by Gill Guile

Brimax · Newmarket · England

The Wind in the Willows

When Mole deserts his underground home for the sunshine and fresh air of the world above, his whole life changes. He makes friends with the Water Rat, learns about the Wild Wood, meets the elusive Badger and of course, Toad!

Contents

The River Bank

Mole had been spring-cleaning all morning. Suddenly he threw down his brush and said, "Bother! Oh blow!" And he bolted out of the house and up the tunnel that led to the sunlight and the great meadow.

He walked until he came to the edge of a river. It was the first time he had ever seen a river. A small, brown face with whiskers was looking at him from a hole in the river bank. It was Water Rat.

"Come for a row on the river," said Rat. "There's nothing better than messing about in boats." Rat put a picnic basket into a little boat, and they set off.

"What place is that?" asked Mole.

"The Wild Wood," said Rat with a shudder.

They waved to Badger, but he took no notice.

Otter came and had a chat. "Toad's out in his new boat," he said.

The sun was beginning to go down when Rat headed for home. Mole wanted to try to row the boat. He couldn't quite get the hang of it and he tipped them both into the river.

"Help!" cried Mole. "I can't swim!"

Rat rescued him and dried him out.

"I think you had better come and stay with me for a while," said Rat. "Then I can teach you about the river."

The Open Road

"Will you take me to meet Mr. Toad?" asked Mole one morning.

"Certainly," said Rat. "We'll walk along to Toad Hall."

"Hooray!" said Toad when he saw them arrive. "Just the animals I wanted to see. I have something I want to show you."

Standing in the stable yard was a gypsy caravan.

"We're going on a trip," said Toad. "Everything is ready."

Rat said he wasn't going ANYWHERE with Toad. Then he saw how much Mole wanted to go, and he changed his mind.

That night they all slept in the caravan. The next morning, they hitched up the horse to the caravan and set off along the road. They were travelling happily along when they heard a noise behind them. Poop! Poop! Whoosh!!! Suddenly there was a blast of wind and a whirl of sound as a motor car roared past them and sped off into the distance.

The horse was so startled that she reared up. With a terrible crash, the caravan fell into a ditch. It was wrecked.

Rat jumped about in the road, shaking his fists. Mole tried to soothe the frightened horse.

Toad sat in the middle of the dusty road murmuring, "Poop, poop... that's the only way to travel...poop, poop..."

"Stop being so silly, Toad," said Mole.

"I give up," said Rat.

They found someone to look after the horse and travelled home by train. The next day, Rat had some very startling news to tell Mole. Toad had bought himself a very large and very expensive motor car.

The Wild Wood

Rat always slept a great deal in the winter. One winter day when Rat was sleeping, Mole decided to go off on his own and explore the Wild Wood. Mole still hadn't met Badger. He hoped he might bump into him there. At first it was fun being in the Wild Wood. But as darkness fell, the wood became very still. Little, narrow faces with hard eyes began to look out from the shadows. Mole was frightened.

Suddenly Mole heard strange whistling and pattering noises. Now Mole really was afraid. Mole began to run. First in one direction and then in the other. He was completely lost in the Wild Wood. He hid in the hollow of an old beech tree, and all around him he could hear whistling and pattering.

When Rat woke up and saw that Mole wasn't at home, he went looking for him. He followed Mole's footprints into the Wild Wood.

"Mole, Mole, where are you? It's me, it's old Rat!"

It was a long time before Rat heard Mole answer him.

"Is that really you, Ratty?" called Mole from the hollow of the tree.

Rat quickly found the beech tree where Mole was hiding, and he crept in beside him. There they stayed until Mole felt brave enough to carry on.

When they came out of the hollow, it was snowing. Everything was covered in a thick, white blanket. Rat thought he knew the way home, but everything looked so different in the snow. Soon he was lost, too.

Then Mole tripped over something. It was a doorscraper.

Rat began scooping away at the snow. He knew that where there was a doorscraper, there was bound to be a door.

"We are saved!" shouted Rat. "It's Badger's door!"

Mr. Badger

"Hang on to the bell, Mole," said Rat as he banged on the door with his stick.

"Who is there?" asked a gruff voice.

"It's me, Rat, and my friend Mole," called Rat. "We have lost our way in the snow."

The door opened. "Come along in," said Badger kindly. He took their wet coats and boots and made them some supper.

"Any news of Toad and his new car?" asked Badger when supper was eaten.

"He's going from bad to worse," said Rat. "He had another smash–up last week. That's the seventh one!"

"He's been in hospital three times," said Mole.

"He'll be killed if we don't do something," said Rat.

"When the time is right we WILL do something," said Badger. "And then we will stand no nonsense."

Rat and Mole stayed at Badger's house that night. The next day, Badger let them use his secret underground tunnels that took them to the edge of the Wild Wood. From there it was easy to find their way home.

Mr. Toad Again

One bright, sunny morning just after summer had started, there was a knock on Rat's front door. It was Badger.

"The hour has come," said Badger.

"Whose hour?" asked Rat anxiously.

"Toad's, of course!" said Mole excitedly.

"We must go to Toad Hall," said Badger.

They arrived at Toad Hall just as Toad came out to get into his shiny, new motor car.

"You're going nowhere," said Badger sternly, and he marched Toad back inside Toad Hall. He sat him down and talked to him VERY seriously, but it didn't do any good. Toad would not promise Badger anything. So on Badger's orders, Rat and Mole locked Toad in his bedroom. And there he stayed for days and days with someone on guard outside the door all the time.

"I do feel ill," moaned Toad one morning when it was Rat's turn to be on guard.

"I'll fetch the doctor," said Rat, and he ran off to the village leaving Toad unguarded. This was just what Toad wanted.

He didn't waste a moment. He leapt out of bed, made a rope with knotted sheets, and escaped through the window.

"Oh, what a clever Toad I am to trick old Rat like that," he sang as he hopped and skipped along the road.

Toad stopped to have dinner at an inn. He could hardly believe his eyes. In the inn yard was the motor car of his dreams.

Toad only meant to look at the car, but somehow he found himself sitting in it. And then, somehow, he found himself driving it.

"Stop, thief, stop!" shouted voices behind Toad.

Toad pretended not to hear.

Toad's Adventures

Toad was caught of course, and put into prison. He cried many tears.

The man who was in charge of the prison had a kind daughter. She felt sorry for Toad. She asked the woman, who did all the prisoners' washing to swap places with Toad, so that he could escape. When Toad was dressed up in the washerwoman's clothes, he thought he WAS the washerwoman.

"Oh, what a clever Toad I am," he sang as the prison gates clanged shut behind him.

When Toad tried to get onto a train, the Station Master wouldn't let him on without a ticket.

"What's wrong?" asked the train driver when he saw Toad walking sadly away.

"I'm a poor washerwoman," cried Toad. "I've lost my money. I can't buy a ticket to get home."

"You can ride up here with me," said the train driver, and he helped Toad up beside him.

When Toad got off the train, he came to a canal. As he walked along beside it, a barge sailed by.

"Good morning!" called the bargewoman to Toad, who was still dressed as the washerwoman.

"Not for me," answered Toad. "I'm a poor washerwoman trying to get to my daughter's house. She lives close by Toad Hall. I've lost all my money and I must walk there."

"You can ride with me," said the bargewoman, "and you can do some washing for me at the same time."

"I suppose anyone can do washing," said Toad to himself, and he got to work with the soap. But he kept on losing it, and his back ached. As he made more and more mess, he became more and more angry.

"You've never washed a thing in your life," laughed the bargewoman.

Toad lost his temper. "Of course I haven't!" he shouted. "I'm Toad! Highly respected Toad!"

The bargewoman looked more closely at Toad.

"Why, so you are!" she said. "I don't want a horrible, crawly toad on my nice, clean barge." She picked Toad up by his leg and threw him into the water. He landed with a big splash!

Toad was furious. He climbed out of the water and untied the horse which pulled the barge along. Then he jumped onto the horse's back and galloped off across the fields.

"Oh, what a clever Toad I am," he shouted.

Toad sold the horse to a gypsy for six shillings and sixpence, and the gypsy gave him as much of his stew as he could eat.

Some time later, Toad came to the road again. He heard a familiar sound. Poop! Poop! It was a motor car. He decided to stop the motor car and ask for a lift.

As Toad stepped into the road, he turned very pale. It was the same motor car that he had stolen! Toad remembered the prison. He sat on the ground and began to cry. He had forgotten that he was still dressed as the washerwoman.

"Oh dear, how sad," said a voice. "Here's a poor, old washerwoman. She's fainted in the road. We must take her to the nearest village."

Soon Toad forgot he was supposed to be a washerwoman.

"Please sir, may I drive your motor car?" he asked the man.

The people in the car were surprised that a washerwoman wanted to drive a motor car. But they decided to let her.

All would have been well if Toad hadn't driven faster and faster and faster! But he couldn't help himself. He couldn't help shouting either.

"Ho! Ho! I am Toad! I am Toad the motor snatcher!"

Everyone jumped onto Toad at the same time. Toad lost his grip on the wheel and the motor car drove straight into a pond.

Toad found himself flying through the air again. This time he landed with a thump on the grass. Everyone else was still in the car, in the pond.

"Oh, what a clever Toad I am," sang Toad as he picked himself up and started to run.

Then Toad heard someone shouting, "Stop, thief! Stop, thief!" He was being chased again.

Toad began to panic. He didn't know where he was running. Suddenly the ground fell away beneath his feet. He was falling into the water.

It was at that moment he saw Rat. He had fallen into the river.

The Return of Toad

Rat gripped Toad by the scruff of his neck and pulled him to safety.

"Go and change out of those silly clothes," said Rat as soon as they were indoors.

Toad told Rat about his adventures and how clever he had been. Then he said, "I think I'll go home to Toad Hall now."

"Haven't you heard?" asked Rat.

"Heard what?" asked Toad.

"When you didn't come home, Badger and Mole moved into Toad Hall to take care of things for you. But the stoats and weasels from the Wild Wood chased them out and took over Toad Hall."

"Oh, have they indeed!" said Toad, picking up a stick. "I'll soon put a stop to that."

Toad marched off to Toad Hall, but he was soon back at Rat's house. He had been shot at and almost squashed by a falling rock. He would need some help if he was to get the stoats and weasels out of Toad Hall.

Then Badger and Mole arrived. Everyone began talking at the same time, trying to decide what they should do.

"Be quiet! All of you!" ordered Badger. "I have a plan."

Badger knew of a secret underground passage that led right under Toad Hall. He had heard that the stoats and weasels were going to have a party the next night. Badger said that they could sneak along the passage under Toad Hall while the party was going on. Then they would attack when the stoats and weasels were least expecting it.

The next night, Toad, Rat, Badger and Mole were ready. The time to chase the stoats and weasels from Toad Hall had arrived. Badger gave each of them a big stick in case they were attacked. Then he took the lantern and led the way along the river bank and into the secret passage.

"We are right under Toad Hall now," whispered Badger.

They could hear the stoats and weasels stamping and cheering overhead. They moved quietly along the passage until they came to a trap door. It opened into the butler's pantry. Now they were in Toad Hall!

The noise from the party was very loud.

Badger puffed himself up. He looked very big and very fierce.

"Follow me!" he shouted.

Badger, Toad, Mole and Rat burst into the party. They shouted and screeched at the stoats and weasels, waving big sticks in the air. There were only four of them, but the stoats and weasels didn't know that. They panicked and fled with squeals of fear. They disappeared through the windows, up the chimney and out of the doors – anywhere to get away from those big sticks.

Soon it was over. The stoats and weasels had gone, and Toad was back where he belonged – in Toad Hall.

Toad knew he had a lot to thank his friends for. He knew he had to stop his silly ways. And from that day onwards he was a changed Toad.